D1389360

For
Ben

First published 2007 by Walker Books Ltd
87 Vauxhall Walk, London SE11 5HJ

2 4 6 8 10 9 7 5 3 1

© 2007 Lucy Cousins
Lucy Cousins font © 2007 Lucy Cousins
The moral rights of the author/illustrator have been asserted

Maisy™. Maisy is a registered trademark of Walker Books Ltd, London.

Printed in China

All rights reserved

British Library Cataloguing in Publication Data:
a catalogue record for this book is available from the British Library

ISBN 978-1-4063-0031-4

www.walkerbooks.co.uk

Maisy's Amazing Big Book of Words

Lucy Cousins

WALKER BOOKS
AND SUBSIDIARIES
LONDON · BOSTON · SYDNEY · AUCKLAND

Getting dressed

t-shirt

socks

trousers

dress

jumper

hat

vest

gloves

coat

pants

shoes

In Maisy's house

light

television

window

table

chair

Cactus

bookshelf

fireplace

sofa

Best friends

charley

Tallulah

Robin

Ostrich

Little
Black
cat

Panda

Cyril

Eddie

On the farm

hay bales

tractor

sheepdog

trailer

muck

egg basket

water trough

pig

piglet

hen house

farm truck

chicks

apple tree

horseshoe

goose

wheat

stable

goat

horse   foal

sheep

lamb

gate

scarecrow

combine harvester

poo

bull

milk churn

maize

Things that go

bus

pushchair

motorbike

car

fire engine

lorry

train

bicycle

Busy
Maisy

scissors

ladder

iron

hammer

nails

screws

screwdriver

Vacuum cleaner

broom

dustpan and brush

Washing line

Making music

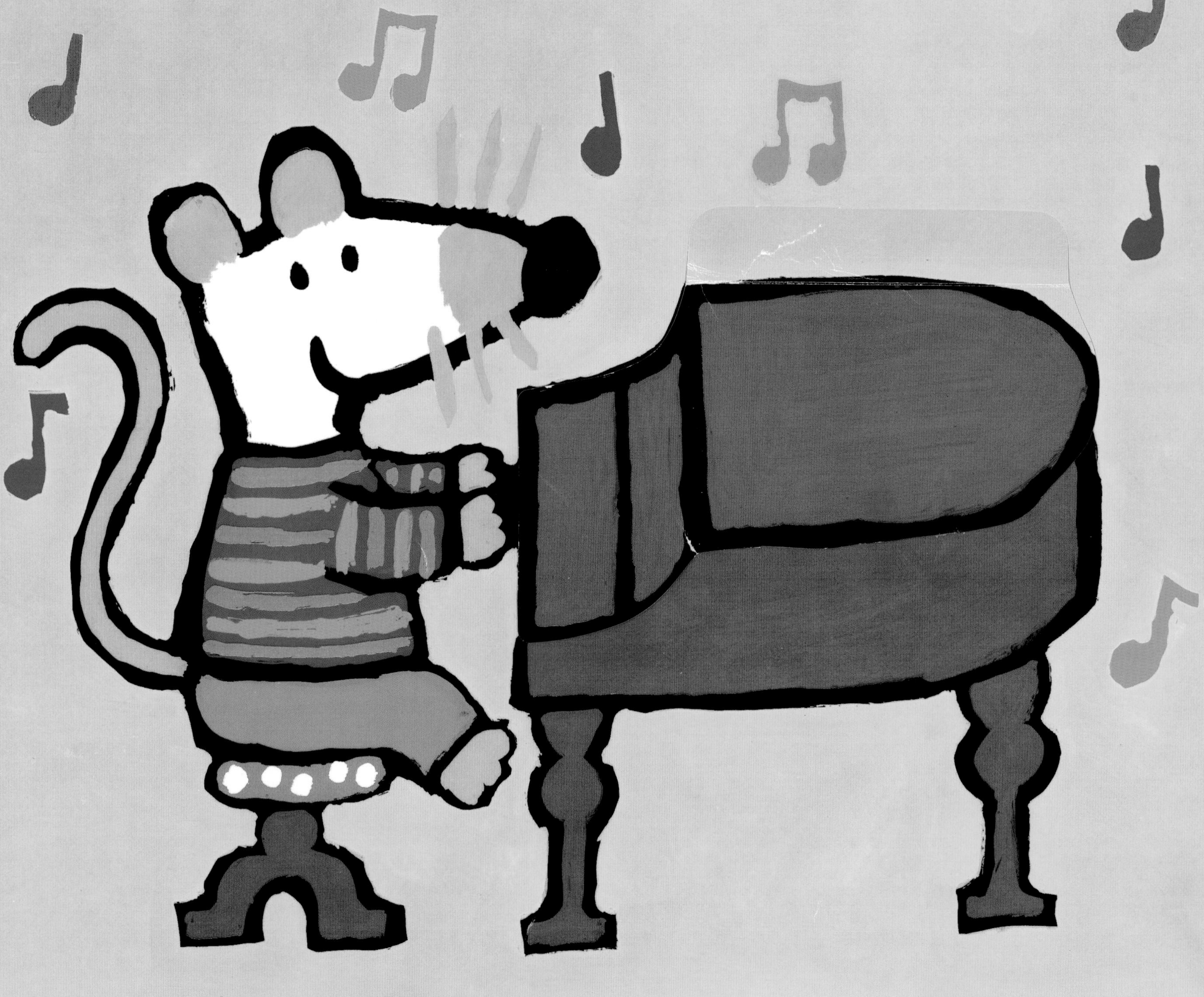

drum

trumpet

xylophone

violin

tambourine

triangle

recorder

guitar

In Maisy's garden

deckchair

beetle

barbecue

bird house

nest

garden
fork

caterpillar

Sandpit

mole

trowel

trike

centipede

wheelbarrow

flowerpot

slug

vegetable patch

shed

ants

leaf

rake

blackbird

hedgehog

daisies

bird table

trampoline

grass

maisy
likes
playing

Toy box

jigsaw

castle

crayons

doll

toy truck

push horse

pram

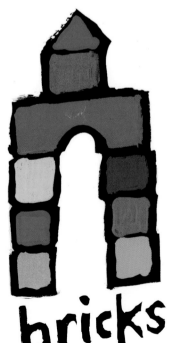

bricks

cuddly bunny

ball

paint box

It's noisy

nee-nah nee-nah nee-nah

la-la-de-da-da

radio

vrooooooooom

aeroplane

tick-tock
tick-tock

clock

vzzzzzzzzz

drill

bring
bring

telephone

brrmmmm
brmmmmm

lawn mower

hee-haw
hee-haw

donkey

Favourite pets

dog

guinea pig

parrot

hamster

stick
insect

fish

pony

Rainy days

frog

lightning

ducklings

umbrella

wellies

worm

puddle

snail

Happy birthday, Maisy

 card

 candles

birthday cake

 balloon

 party food

 party clothes

 Sweets

party bag

 jelly

 paper hat

 party blower

  presents

In the sea

octopus

starfish

turtle

whale

jellyfish

fish

shrimp

seaweed

seahorse

dolphin

maisy
loves
animals

lion

toucan

koala

butterfly

tortoise

grasshopper

tiger

lemur

flamingo

snake

penguin

polar bear

kangaroo

leopard

hippopotamus

swan

puffin

peacock

giraffe

zebra

On the beach

cowboy

king

fairy

fire fighter

pirate

doctor

Let's cook

saucepan

jug

rolling pin

mixer

teapot

sieve

sink

jam

flour

cookbook

colander

lemon

lemon squeezer

whisk

scales

coffee pot

eggs

butter

wooden spoon

plate

measuring cup

sugar

bowl

toaster

kettle

grater

knife and fork

glass

jam tarts

Sunny days

sunglasses

bee

toy boat

hot-air balloon

sunhat

dragonfly

ice lolly

lemonade

flowers

sun cream

In the park

slide

kite

skateboard

rocking horse

pond

tennis racket

football

seesaw

swings

Yum, yum!

apple

carrot

biscuits

egg

banana

yogurt

grapes

broccoli

spaghetti

milk

orange

sundae

beans

tomato

pineapple

peas

cheese

sandwich

strawberries

bread

juice

Bathtime

scrubbing
brush

soap

rubber
duck

towel

shampoo

Washing
basket

plug

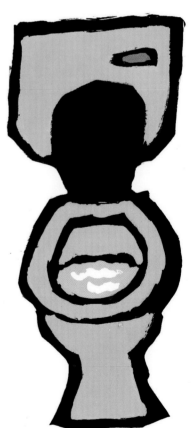
toilet

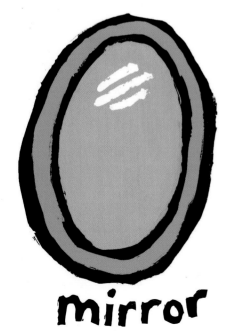
mirror

comb

Bedtime

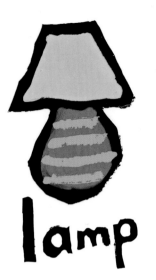
lamp

moon

toothbrush

pyjamas

alarm
clock

dressing gown

book

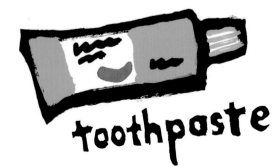
toothpaste

slippers

stars

owl